**This Way
To
MY OWN PICTURE
DIARY**

Printed in Hong Kong

Illustrations were created by JoAnn DeJoria Smith
copyright © 1974, 1993 & 2001 JoAnn DeJoria Smith

ISBN Number 0 9715405-1-9

Published by:
Sonrose Publishers

Sold and Licensed to the trade by:
Global Publishing Services
6487 NW Lamonta Road
Prineville, Oregon 97754-8230

1974, 1993 & 2001
by JoAnn DeJoria Smith

The
Alphabuddies™

A Note From JoAnn DeJoria Smith

These letters were born in New York City in 1974 after a tragedy in my life. My husband had died in a motorcycle accident, and a year later I was visiting New York. I wanted to make our daughter a birthday card. So I went into an art store in Manhattan and bought a few art supplies, and that is when I drew my first letters which became The Alphabuddies.

Twenty-seven years later, I was working on My Own Picture Dairy, the first completed Alphabuddies project, when the World Trade Center and Pentagon were attacked. I wanted to do something to help the children, so I spoke with John Paul DeJoria and asked if he would donate some of these Picture Diaries to charity. A crisis counselor in New York told me the books would be a useful tool for therapy with children in any counseling situation.

I am delighted to be able to make MY OWN PICTURE DIARY available not only as a gift book but also as a counseling tool for children in crisis. I hope this book will serve as a keepsake for those who are treasuring their good times, and a healing tool for those who are going through life's rough places.

And a word to children -- if you have a dream, don't let it die just because of what someone has told you, or a poor grade on a report card. After getting a D in art class, I had no confidence to draw. However, a few people encouraged me to keep drawing my letters, and a dream began to form in my heart to make books using The Alphabuddies. I'm glad I ignored the voices of those who said I couldn't do it.

This picture diary is dedicated in loving memory of my
husband, Bob DeJoria, who was only with us on this earth 29 years.
Also to our precious daughter, Heather Lynn Hutchens, and
our first grandson, Robert Huston Hutchens, born October 16, 2001.
Dad would have been so proud of both of you.

With Much Love,

MOM

(aka Grandma)

THE ALPHABUDDIES

This Diary Belongs To:

_____

A Gift From: _____

Date: _____

Occasion: _____

A Special Note For You: _____

_____

_____

_____

_____

_____

ALPHABUDDIES

ALPHABUDDIES

ALPHABUDDIES

THE ALPHABUDDIES

A B C D E F G
H I J K L M N
O P Q R S T U
V W X Y Z

ALPHABUDDIES

ALPHABUDDIES

ALPHABUDDIES

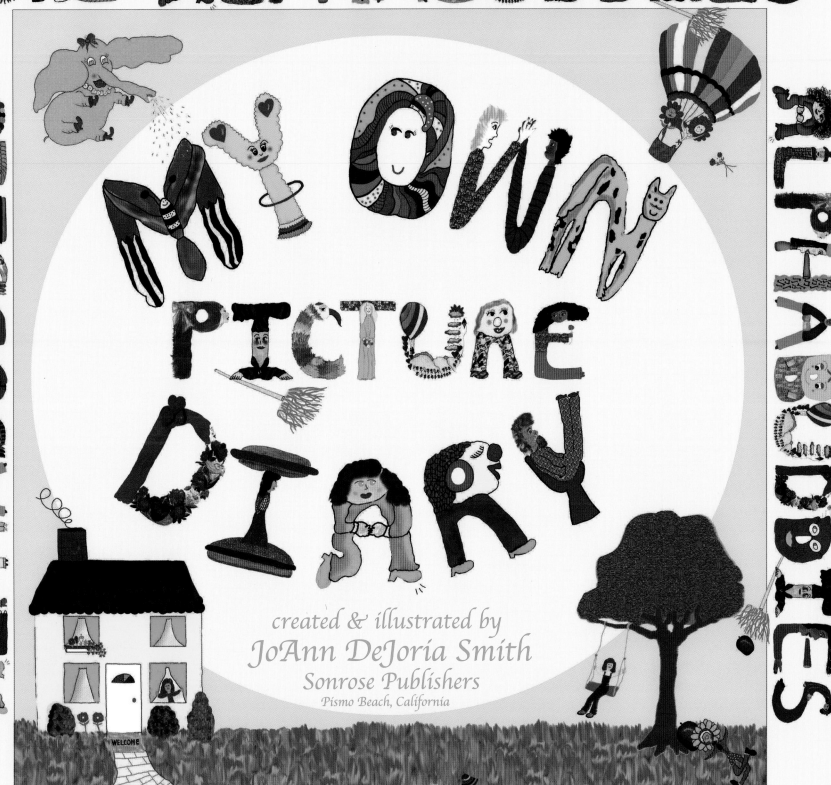

THE ALPHABUDDIES

MY OWN
PICTURE
DIARY

created & illustrated by
JoAnn DeJoria Smith
Sonrose Publishers
Pismo Beach, California

ALPHABUDDIES

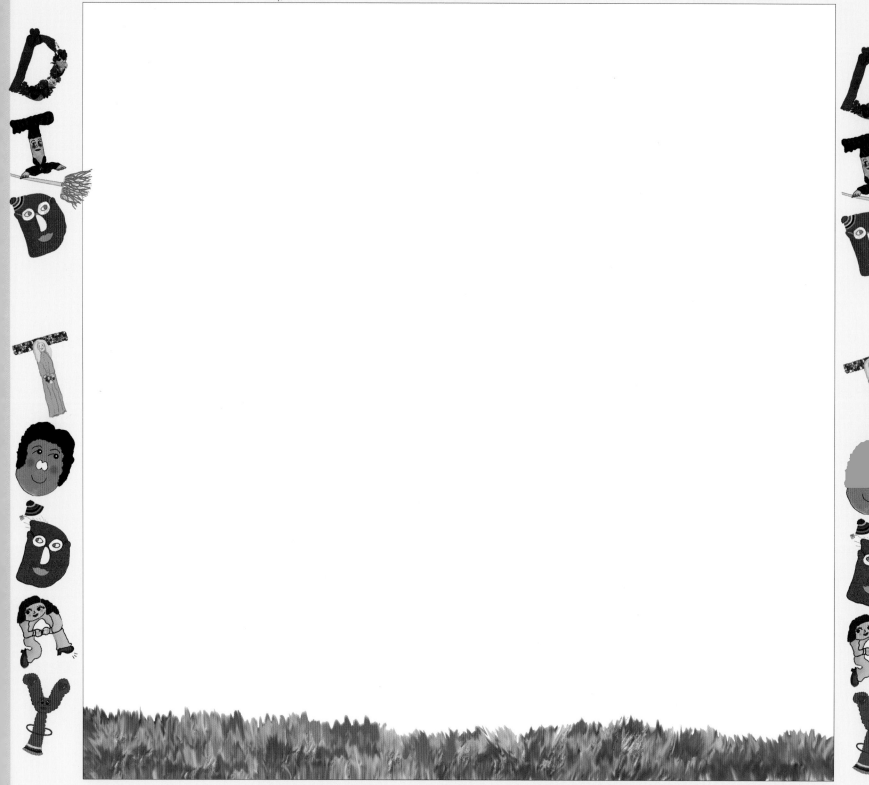

Notes:

Date:

Notes:

Date:

Notes:

DRAW WHERE YOU LIVE

Notes:

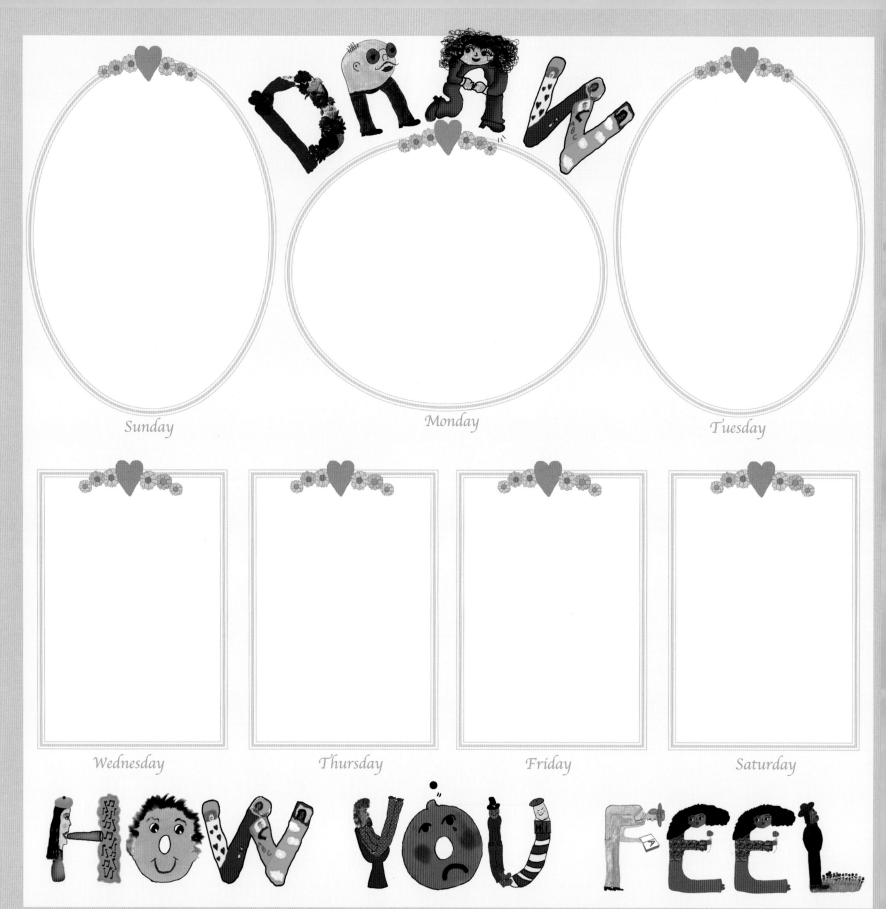

Sunday

Monday

Tuesday

Wednesday

Thursday

Friday

Saturday

Week of:

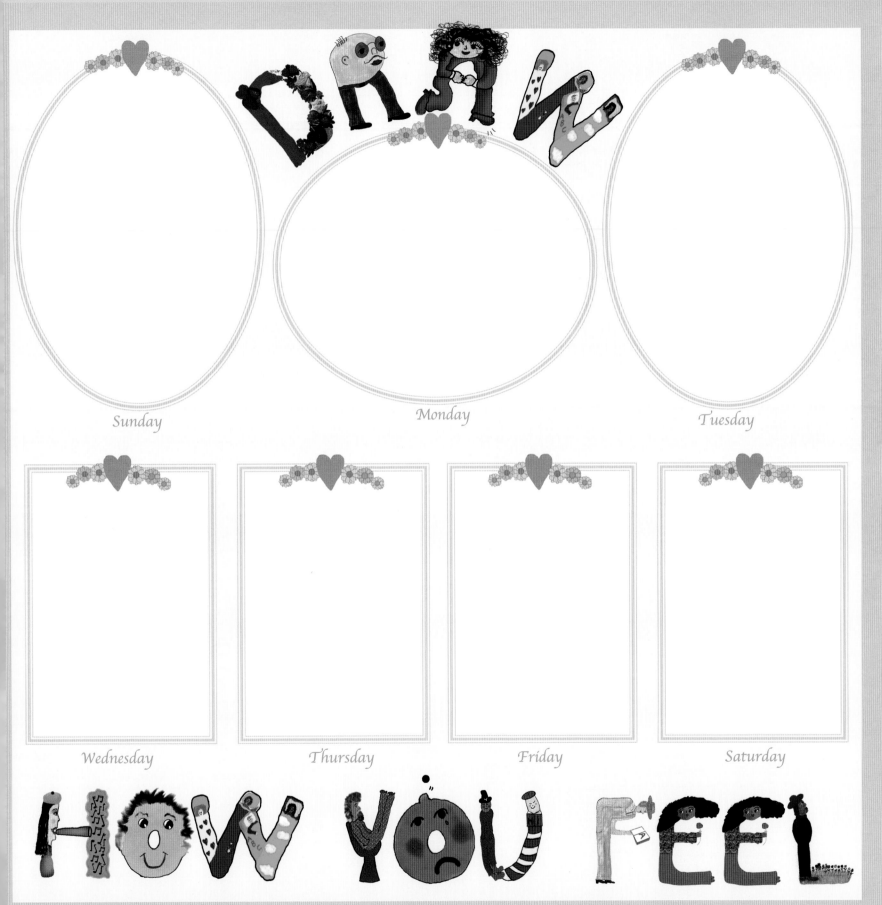

Sunday

Monday

Tuesday

Wednesday

Thursday

Friday

Saturday

Week of:

DRAW A PICTURE

Notes:

DRAW A PICTURE

Notes:

Notes:

Date:

Notes:

Date:

DRAW A SECRET PLACE

Date:

Notes:

Date:

Notes:

Date:

DRAW A SPECIAL PLACE

Notes:

Date:

DRAW SOMETHING SILLY

Notes:

Date:

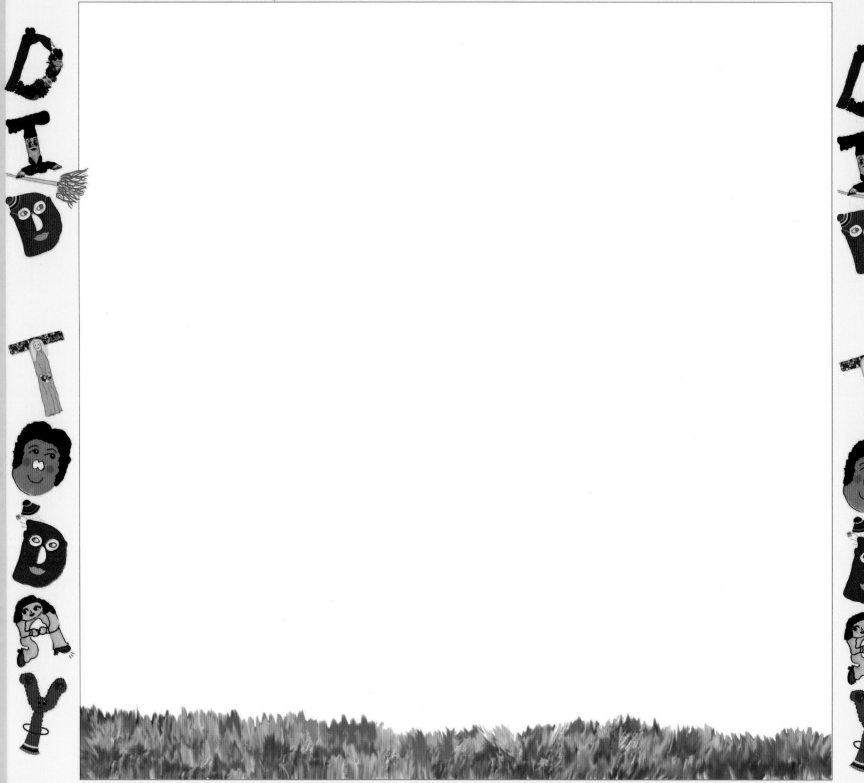

Notes: Date:

Notes: Date:

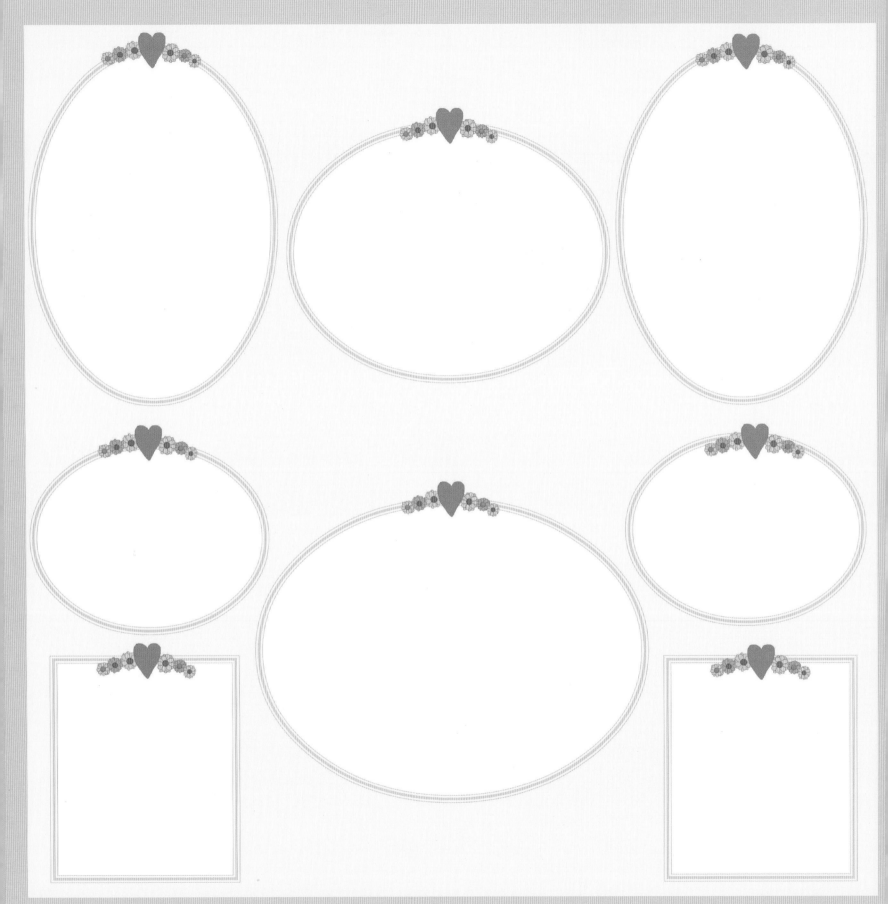

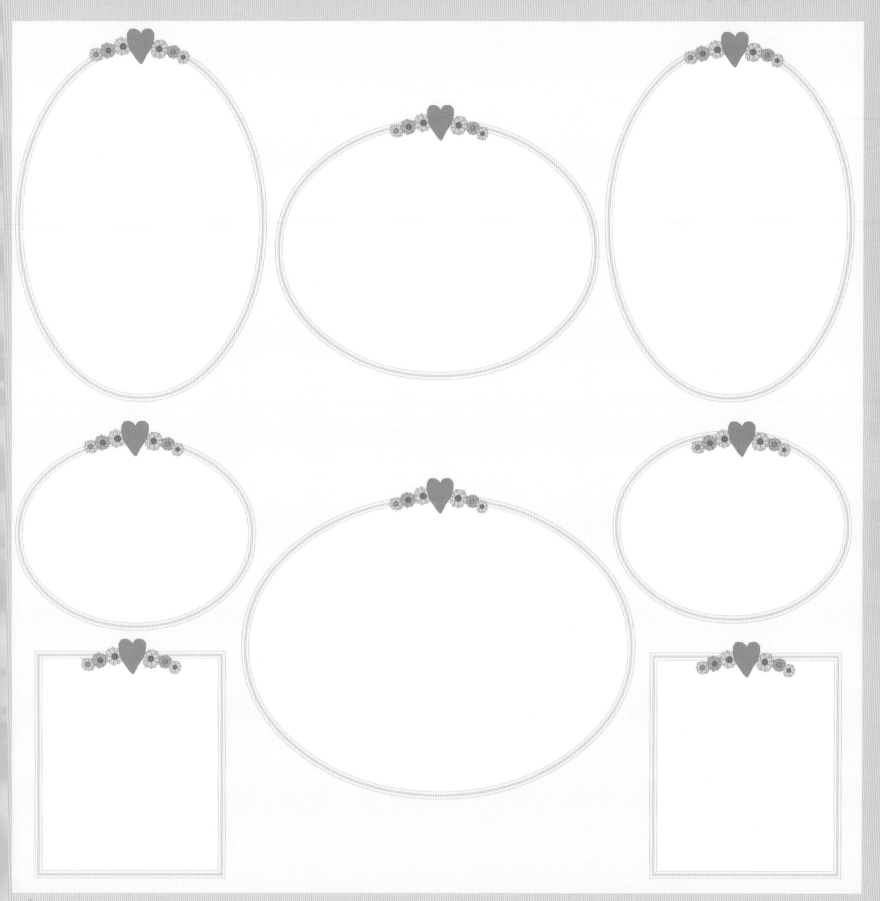

Notes:

Notes:

DRAW MOUNTAINS

Date:

DRAW A SUNRISE

Notes:

DRAW A TREE

Notes:

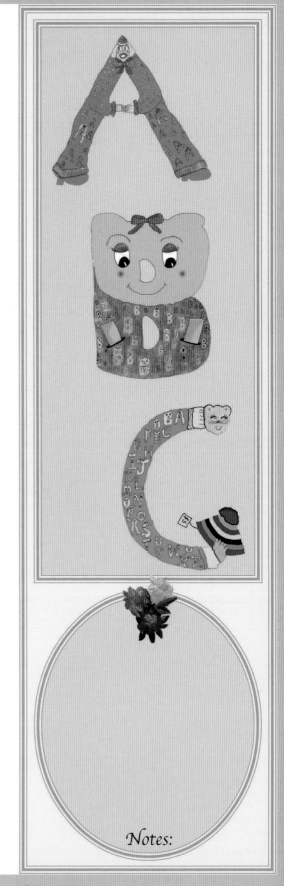

Notes:

Date:

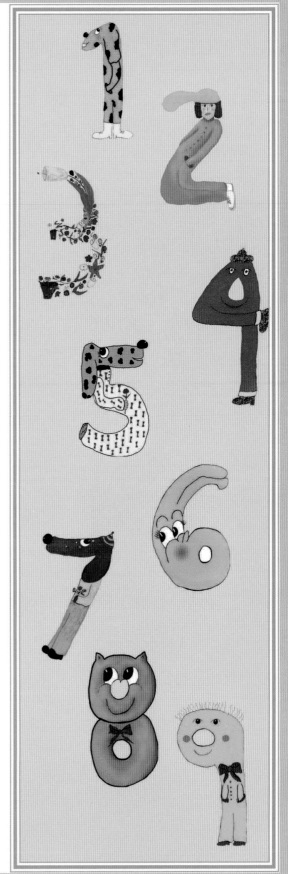

Notes:

DRAW YOUR FAVORITE GAME

Notes: